Purr-im Time!

by Jenna Waldman

illustrated by Erica J. Chen

APPLES & HONEY PRESS

To Pippa, Midnight, & Margot. — J.W.

To all the kitties—it's not you, it's my allergies. — E.J.C.

Apples & Honey Press
An Imprint of Behrman House Publishers
Millburn, New Jersey 07041
www.applesandhoneypress.com

ISBN 978-1-68115-593-7

Library of Congress Cataloging-in-Publication Data
Names: Waldman, Jenna, author. | Chen, Erica J., illustrator.
Title: Purr-im time / by Jenna Waldman ; illustrated by Erica Chen.
Description: Millburn, New Jersey : Apples & Honey Press, [2023] | Summary:
  "Kitties celebrate Purim and get up to shenanigans."
Identifiers: LCCN 2021049633 | ISBN 9781681155937 (hardcover)
Subjects: CYAC: Stories in rhyme. | Cats--Fiction. |
  Animals--Infancy--Fiction. | Purim--Fiction. | LCGFT: Stories in rhyme.
  | Picture books.
Classification: LCC PZ8.3.W145 Pu 2023 | DDC [E]--dc23
LC record available at https://lccn.loc.gov/2021049633

Design by Marell Creative Services
Edited by Alef Davis
Printed in China

The illustrations in this book were created using digital techniques. The artist sketched directly on the computer with a pen tablet, then finalized the art by adding digital brushstrokes, patterns, and textures.

9 8 7 6 5 4 3 2 1

One eye opens, then another.
Purr-im time is here!

Kitties wake from cozy dozing.
Purr-im time is here!

In the kitchen, kitties mix
the hamantaschen dough.

Roll it thin and slice the circles.
Lay them in a row.

Cookies filled with gooey fruit
are shaped like Haman's hat.

Kitties think they look like ears.

"Oh no! "

"Mee-ow! "

Kersplat!

Furry bellies
fill with goodies,

tongues find
every crumb.

Little paws are drippy-sticky,
lick the sweetness—yum!

Box up treats and tasty sweets:
a Purr-im nosh to share.

Kindness marks this special day;
the kitties show they care.

Kitties wearing
festive costumes
leap in the parade.

Capes and
crowns,
and flowing
gowns, and
one bejeweled
*meow*maid.

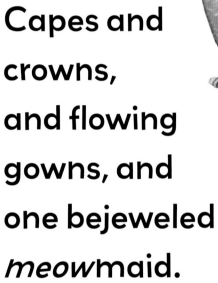

Whiskers wiggle, kitties giggle;
"Chag Purr-im!" they call.
Rainbow-colored streamers wave,
confetti starts to fall.

Time for the *megillah* reading!
Gather round to hear
the story of how brave Queen
Esther overcomes her fear.

Wicked Haman causes trouble.
"Boooo!" the kitties shout.
Grab a gragger, maybe two,
and shake them all about!

Haman wants to hurt the Jews;

his heart is
full of spite.

No one else can save her people—
Esther leads the fight!

She warns the king of Haman's plot;
the kitties shout, "Hooray!"

All it takes is one strong voice—
Queen Esther saves the day.

The carnival is packed with games and prizes to be won. Don't forget to give tzedakah—helping out is fun.

Pouncing-bouncing, kitties cheer
and flash their toothy smiles.

But tails are trippy,
costumes slippy—
kitties land in piles.

The day of play is winding down;
the kitties start to scrub.

And when they've finished cleaning up,
they topple in the tub.

Sleepy kitties, purring-peaceful,
curl up head-to-head.

Sneaky kitty hides a treat
to chomp when she's in bed.

One eye closes, then another.
Purr-im time was here!

Kitties dream of what they'll do
when Purr-im comes next year!

A Note for Families

The kitties love celebrating Purim together. Working as a team, they bake hamantaschen, have a parade, and put on a play. Even cleaning up is fun because they do it together.

Just as Queen Esther looked out for her people, the kitties show they care by delivering packages of food to friends, family, and those in need. These packages are called *mishlo'ach manot* and help everyone feel included in the Purim celebration. Even one small mitzvah of giving can make a big difference in our communities. Follow the steps below to create your own festive package of Purim treats to share.

Mishlo'ach Manot Craft

Supplies

- small cardboard box
- colorful paper
- pencil
- scissors
- glue or double-sided tape
- markers
- ribbon, stickers, feathers, and other decorative items
- Purim treats
- tissue paper

Directions

1. Trace the sides of the box onto your paper with the pencil and cut out the shapes to fit.
2. Using glue or double-sided tape, attach the shapes to the outside of the box.
3. Decorate the box with markers, ribbon, feathers, stickers, etc.
4. Write a special note for the recipient.
5. Place Purim treats, the note, and tissue paper in the box.
6. Seal the box with tape and/or ribbon and deliver!

CHAG PURR-IM